MW00886171

Xwáy, Xwáy and the Giant Red Cedar

Story by Zulebia Esmail

Illustrations by Laura Catrinella

With special thanks to Maricella
Pineda and Ishtar Esmail

◆ FriesenPress

Suite 300 - 990 Fort St
Victoria, BC, V8V 3K2
Canada

www.friesenpress.com

ISBN
978-1-5255-6325-6 (Hardcover)
978-1-5255-6326-3 (Paperback)
978-1-5255-6327-0 (eBook)

1. JUVENILE FICTION, PEOPLE & PLACES, CANADA, NATIVE CANADIAN

Distributed to the trade by The Ingram Book Company

According to legend, the Western Red Cedar is a very special tree gifted by the Great Spirit to the earliest people of British Columbia. The people used this tree for many things in their lives, including making houses and tools and using its oils to repel insects. XwáýXwáý (pronounced **Whoi whoi**) was a real Indigenous village located at present day Lumberman's Arch in Stanley Park, Vancouver, British Columbia.

But how did the people figure out all the things that the Western Red Cedar tree could be used for?

Set out on a great adventure with two young boys to find out.

A long time ago, two twin boys named Xwáý
(pronounced **Whoi**) and Xwáý lived in a place that is
now known as Stanley Park. Everyday, Father went
searching for food **(foraging)** and didn't come home
until the shadows grew long. It was hard work for
him, as he didn't have hunting tools. Xwáý and Xwáý
were too young to help him, so they stayed home with
their mother.

Question: What can Father bring home to eat?

Answer: Eggs, acorns, berries, edible mushrooms, dandelions, sunflowers, fiddleheads, and grouse.

Skills: Inferential Comprehension; Vocabulary

One day, when the boys were older, Father sat Xwáỷ and Xwáỷ down after supper and said, "You are both grown now, and it is time for you to go on a Quest."

"What is a Quest?" asked Xwáỷ.

Father explained, "It is a great adventure that you must make to seek knowledge and…"

Xwáỷ's brother, Xwáỷ, interrupted. "But how will we know what kind of knowledge we are looking for, and what will we do with it?"

Father replied patiently, "The knowledge you gain must benefit our people. Once you have it, you can come back and share it with all of us."

The next day, the twins said "good-bye" to their parents and set out on their Quest.

Question: What animals did the twins see in the forest?

Answer: Raccoons, moose, coyotes, woodpeckers, Canada geese, ducks, squirrels

Skills: Inferential Comprehension; Vocabulary

After walking for many kilometres, they found some wild raspberry bushes. Nearby, a Spirit Bear slurped on some honeycomb hanging from a big, beautiful tree.

Xwáy̓ looked at it with envy. "Honey is so yummy. I wish we could take it home."

His brother lamented, "But we can't carry it in our hands."

The Spirit Bear boomed in his deep voice, "The Giant Red Cedar has a very special bark that tears into long strips. I would be happy to show you how to make baskets with it."

The Giant Red Cedar smiled. "I am one of a kind, but I will share my bark with you. In return, I ask that you plant my seed cone, so I will have more of my kind."

Question: What will the twins do now? What will happen next?

Skill: Predicting (Sequence of Events)

A few days later, the boys continued on their Quest with a basket of berries and honeycomb. They were so excited about what they had learned that they forgot to plant the seed cone.

As they walked along the shoreline, they watched a Bald Eagle catch fish. "If we had sharp talons like that bold eagle, we could catch fish easily," said Xwáy̓.

His brother agreed, "It would be very useful for our people."

The Bald Eagle saw and heard them with his sharp eyes and ears and swooped down. "The branches of the Giant Red Cedar are tough and flexible. I can teach you how to make hunting tools with them."

Xwáy̓ and Xwáy̓ returned to the Giant Red Cedar, who smiled indulgently at them. "I am one of a kind, but I will share my branches with you. In return, I ask that you plant my seed cone, so I will have more of my kind."

Question: What kind of hunting tools can the twins make with the branches?

Question: "Bald" means lacking hair and "bold" means fearless. Why is this kind of bird called a bald eagle?

Skills: Recognizing Possibilities; Critical Thinking

After many days on their Quest, the boys were walking along a river when Xwáý said excitedly, "We can go home now and share how to make things from the Giant Red Cedar."

His brother eagerly agreed. "I wish we could get home quickly."

The Beaver heard them and slapped his tail to get their attention. "The wood of the Giant Red Cedar is very unique. It is light, and it does not rot. I can show you how to make a canoe and help you cut the wood." The twins rushed with the Beaver to the Giant Red Cedar.

Question: What do you think the Giant Red Cedar is thinking/feeling?

Skill: Understanding and Predicting the Feelings/Thinking of Others

The Giant Red Cedar grew alarmed at the twins' plan.
"I shared my bark, and I shared my branches with you. I
can share my wood too, but I'm one of a kind, so you must
plant my seed cone, so there will be more of my kind."

The twins accepted the seed cone, and with the Beaver's
help, made a canoe. However, the boys were so excited
to be returning home that they forgot to plant the seed
cone again.

Question: What will happen if Xwáý and Xwáý do not plant the seed cone?

Skills: Cause and Effect; Logical Reasoning

Father and Mother were very happy to see Xwáý and Xwáý and extremely proud of the valuable knowledge they shared. Soon, people made the long journey to see the amazing tree of which the boys spoke.

"Where is the tree with the bark, the branches, and wood?" asked Father.

"I see only this stump!" said Mother sadly.

The Giant Red Cedar was no more. Everyone was disappointed.

Xwáý reached into his satchel basket. "The seed cone!" he said removing it.

His brother remembered, "It is one of a kind, and we have to plant it." The twins promised to honour the Giant Red Cedar.

Question: What would you do to honour the tree?

Skill: Imagination

Xwáý and Xwáý planted the seed cone and watched it slowly grow. Year after year, they checked to see if it had made any new seed cones. They knew they couldn't use the special tree until it had seed cones to make more of its kind.

Xwáý and Xwáý grew older and had families of their own. One day, as Xwáý and Xwáý approached the Red Cedar with their children, Xwáý's little boy yelled, "Papa, the Red Cedar has seed cones."

Xwáý's daughter gushed, "We need to plant them."

Xwáý laughed. "Yes!"

His brother joined in, "We shall plant them first before using the tree."

Xwáý and Xwáý and their children planted the seed cones. Then they used the wood of the Red Cedar to sculpt a beautiful totem pole to remind their people of their vow and to thank the tree for its generosity and all the animals that helped them in their Quest.

Question: What things were made from the Giant Red Cedar?

Question: Can you think of anything else that is made from trees?

Skill: Memory; Comprehension; Expanding Knowledge

Zulebia Esmail lives in Vancouver, British Columbia and enjoys taking walks with her husband and the family dog in Stanley Park, which was once the site of the Indigenous village called Xwáy̓xwáy̓ (pronounced Whoi whoi) that inspired her story.

Zulebia is an Early Childhood Educator and has owned and managed programs for her daycare, preschool and out of school care for thirty years. She notes she wanted to "write a book that sends a mindful message and that is a fun and interactive learning experience that provides an opportunity for parents to assess their children's language abilities and expand knowledge as a family." Xwáy̓, Xwáy̓ and the Giant Red Cedar is her first book.